W9-BXM-516

Pig Kahuna

NEW YORK BERLIN LONDON SYDNEY

First published in the United States of America in May 2011
by Bloomsbury Books for Young Readers
www.bloomsburykids.com

For information about permission to reproduce selections from this book, write to
Permissions, Bloomsbury BFYR, 175 Fifth Avenue, New York, New York 10010

Library of Congress Cataloging-in-Publication Data
Sattler, Jennifer Gordon.
Pig kahuna / by Jennifer Sattler. — 1st U.S. ed.
p. cm.
Summary: Fergus is afraid to go in the water, but he and his baby brother
Dink find a surfboard while collecting treasures along the seashore.
ISBN 978-1-59990-635-5 (hardback) • ISBN 978-1-59990-636-2 (reinforced)
[1. Pigs—Fiction. 2. Surfing—Fiction.] I. Title.
PZ7.S24935Pig 2011 [E]—dc22 2010035629

Art created with acrylics and colored pencil
Typeset in Birdlegs
Book design by Nicole Gastonguay

Printed in China by Toppan Leefung Printing, Ltd., Dongguan, Guangdong
2 4 6 8 10 9 7 5 3 1 (hardcover)
2 4 6 8 10 9 7 5 3 1 (reinforced)

All papers used by Bloomsbury Publishing, Inc., are natural, recyclable products
made from wood grown in well-managed forests. The manufacturing processes
conform to the environmental regulations of the country of origin.

For Paul

It was Saturday. Fergus and his baby brother, Dink, were collecting treasures.

The waves would roll in, leave something for their collection, and roll back out again. It worked quite nicely as long as Fergus didn't have to go in the water.

He knew there was more than
just treasure in that water.

There was a
lurking,
murky
ickiness.

So far that day Fergus and Dink
had collected:

some seaweed,

a pebble that looked
like an eyeball,

and a shell that *might*
be an actual shark's tooth.

And then . . .

They waited fifteen whole minutes, but nobody came to claim the surfboard. So they decided to make it the star of their collection.

Of course, surfing on it was out of the question because of the lurking, murky ickiness factor of the water.

So they found other, drier uses for it.

And they named it Dave.

Dave was a loyal companion. “Stay. Good boy.”

After a while, Fergus offered to get some ice cream. "Chunky chocolate Chattanooga chew-chew chip, right, Dink?"

Dink looked long
and hard at Dave.

He seemed to have lost his shine.

"You miss the ocean, huh, big fella?
You should be wild! And free!"

DAVE!

Fergus ran into the water and
furiously swam out to save Dave.

Bon voyage!

“Don’t worry, little buddy,” he whispered.

“I’ve got you.”

No sooner had the words left
Fergus's mouth than he felt
Dave rise up beneath him.

"Fergus," said Dink, "you surfed!"

"I surfed!"

Fergus and Dink kept their eyes peeled for more treasures.

And, boy, did they find one.